I0823757

THE
HAUNTED BOOKSHELF

he telling or reading of ghost stories during long, dark, and cold Christmas nights is a yuletide ritual dating back to at least the eighteenth century, and was once as much a part of Christmas tradition as decorating fir trees, feasting on goose, and the singing of carols. During the Victorian era many magazines printed ghost stories specifically for the Christmas season. These "winter tales" didn't necessarily explore Christmas themes. Rather, they were offered as an eerie pleasure to be enjoyed on Christmas Eve with the family, adding a supernatural shiver to the seasonal chill.

The tradition remained strong in the British Isles (and her colonies) throughout much of the twentieth century, though in recent years it has been on the wane. Certainly, few people in Canada or the United States seem to know about it any longer. This series of small books seeks to rectify this, to revive a charming custom for the long, dark nights we all know so well here at Christmastime.

Charles Dickens
*The Signalman*

A.M. Burrage
*One Who Saw*

Edith Wharton
*Afterward*

M.R. James
*The Diary of Mr. Poynter*

Marjorie Bowen
*The Crown Derby Plate*

E.F. Benson
*How Fear Departed the Long Gallery*

W.W. Jacobs
*The Toll House*

Algernon Blackwood
*The Empty House*

H. Russell Wakefield
*The Red Lodge*

Frank Cowper
*Christmas Eve on a Haunted Hulk*

R.H. Malden
*The Sundial*

Elizabeth Gaskell
*The Old Nurse's Story*

Daphne du Maurier
*The Apple Tree*

Richard Bridgeman
*The Morgan Trust*

M.R. James
*The Story of a Disappearance and an Appearance*

Walter de la Mare
*The Green Room*

Margaret Oliphant
*The Open Door*

Bernard Capes
*An Eddy on the Floor*

F. Marion Crawford
*The Doll's Ghost*

Edith Wharton
*Mr. Jones*

Shirley Jackson
*A Visit*

Cynthia Asquith
*The Corner Shop*

Gertrude Atherton
*The Dead and the Countess*

Arthur Conan Doyle
*The Captain of the Polestar*

Marjorie Bowen
*The House by the Poppy Field*

Andrew Caldecott
*A Room in a Rectory*

L.P. Hartley
*Podolo*

Laurence Whistler
*Captain Dalgety Returns*

Mary Fitt
*The Amethyst Cross*

Rosemary Timperley
*The Mistress in Black*

Sarah Orne Jewett
*Lady Ferry*

H. Russell Wakefield
*Lucky's Grove*

# LUCKY'S GROVE

H. RUSSELL WAKEFIELD

A GHOST STORY FOR CHRISTMAS

DESIGNED & DECORATED BY SETH

BIBLIOASIS

*"And Loki begat Hel, Goddess of the Grave, Fenris, the Great Wolf, and the Serpent, Nidnogg, who lives beneath The Tree."*

MR BRAXTON STROLLED with his land agent, Curtis, into the Great Barn.

"There you are," said Curtis, in a satisfied tone, "the finest little fir I ever saw, and the kiddies will never set eyes on a lovelier Christmas tree."

Mr Braxton examined it; it stood twenty feet from huge green pot to crisp, straight peak, and was exquisitely sturdy, fresh, and symmetrical.

"Yes, it's a beauty," he agreed. "Where did you find it?"

"In that odd little spinney they call Lucky's Grove, in the long meadow near the river boundary."

"Oh!" remarked Mr Braxton uncertainly. To himself he was saying vaguely, "He shouldn't have got it from there, of course he wouldn't realize it, but he shouldn't have got it from there."

"Of course we'll replant it," said Curtis, noticing his employer's diminished enthusiasm. "It's a curious thing, but it isn't a young tree; it's apparently full-grown. Must be a dwarf variety, but I don't know as much about trees as I should like."

Mr Braxton was surprised to find there was one branch of country lore on which Curtis was not an expert; for he was about the best-known man at his job in the British

Isles. Pigs, bees, chickens, cattle, crops, running a shoot, he had mastered them one and all. He paid him two thousand a year with house and car. He was worth treble.

"I expect it's all right," said Mr Braxton; "it is just that Lucky's Grove is—is—well, 'sacred' is perhaps too strong a word. Maybe I should have told you, but I expect it's all right."

"That accounts for it then," laughed Curtis. "I thought there seemed some reluctance on the part of the men while we were yanking it up and getting it on the lorry. They handled it a bit gingerly; on the part of the older men, I mean, the youngsters didn't worry."

"Yes, there would be," said Mr Braxton. "But never mind, it'll be back in a few days and it's a superb little tree. I'll bring Mrs Braxton along to see it after lunch." And he strolled back into Abingdale Hall.

Fifty-five years ago, Mr Braxton's father had been a labourer on this very estate, and in that year, young Percy, aged eight, had got an errand boy's job in Oxford. Twenty years later he'd owned one small shop. Twenty-five years after that, fifty big shops. Now, though he had finally retired, he owned two hundred and eighty vast shops and was a millionaire whichever way you added it up. How had this happened? No one can quite answer such questions. Certainly he'd worked like a brigade of Trojans, but mid-night oil has to burn in Aladdin's lamp before it can transform ninepence into one million pounds. It was just that he asked no quarter from the unforgiving minute, but squeezed from it the fruit of others' many hours. Those like Mr Braxton seem to have their own time scale; they just say the word and up springs a fine castle of commerce, but the knowledge of that word cannot be imparted; it is as mysterious as the Logos. But all through his great labours he had been moved by one fixed resolve—to avenge his father—that fettered spirit—for he had been an able, intelligent man who had had no earthly chance of revealing the fact to the world. Always the categorical determination had blazed in his son's brain, "I will own Abingdale Hall, and, where my father sweated, I will rule and be lord." And of course it had happened. Fate accepts the dictates of such men as Mr Braxton, shrugs its shoulders, and leaves its revenge to Death. The Hall had come on the market just when he was about to retire, and with an odd delight, an obscure sense of homecoming, the native returned, and his riding boots, shooting boots, golf shoes, and all the many glittering guineas' worth, stamped in and obliterated the prints of his father's hobnails.

That was the picture he often re-visualized, the way it amused him to "put it to himself," as he roamed his broad acres and surveyed the many glowing triumphs of his model husbandry.

Some credit was due to buxom, blithe, and debonair Mrs Braxton, kindly, competent, and innately adaptable. She was awaiting him in the morning room and they went in solitary state to luncheon. But it was the last peaceful lunch they would have for a spell—"the Families" were pouring in on the morrow.

As a footman was helping them to Sole Meunière, Mr Braxton said, "Curtis has found a very fine Christmas tree. It's in the barn. You must come and look at it after lunch."

"That *is* good," replied his wife. "Where did he get it from?"

Mr Braxton hesitated for a moment.

"From Lucky's Grove."

Mrs Braxton looked up sharply.

"From the grove!" she said, surprised.

"Yes, of course he didn't realize—anyway it'll be all right, it's all rather ridiculous, and it'll be replanted before the New Year."

"Oh, yes," agreed Mrs Braxton. "After all it's only just a clump of trees."

"Quite. And it's just the right height for the ballroom. It'll be taken in there tomorrow morning and the electricians will work on it in the afternoon."

"I heard from Lady Pounser just now," said Mrs Braxton. "She's bringing six over, that'll make seventy-four; only two refusals. The presents are arriving this afternoon."

They discussed the pay discursively over the cutlets and Pèche Melba, and soon after lunch walked across to the barn. Mr Braxton waved to Curtis, who was examining a new

tractor in the garage fifty yards away, and he came over.

Mrs Braxton looked the tree over and was graciously delighted with it, but remarked that the pot could have done with another coat of paint. She pointed to several streaks, rust coloured, running through the green. "Of course it won't show when it's wrapped, but they didn't do a very good job."

Curtis leaned down. "They certainly didn't," he answered irritably. "I'll see to it. I think it's spilled over from the soil; that copse is on a curious patch of red sand—there are some at Frilford too. When we pulled it up I noticed the roots were stained a dark crimson." He put his hand down and scraped at the stains with his thumb. He seemed a shade puzzled.

"It shall have another coat at once," he said. "What do you think of Lampson and Colletts' scheme for the barn?"

"Quite good," replied Mrs Braxton, "but the sketches for the chairs are too fancy."

"I agree," said Curtis, who usually did so in the case of unessentials; reserving his tactful vetoes for the others.

The Great Barn was by far the most aesthetically satisfying as it was the oldest feature of the Hall buildings, it was vast, exquisitely proportioned, and mellow. That could hardly be said of the house itself, which the 4th Baron of Abingdale had rebuilt on the cinders of its predecessor in 1752.

This nobleman had travelled abroad extensively and returned with most enthusiastic, grandiose, and indigestible ideas of architecture. The result was a gargantuan piece of rococo-jocoso which only an entirely humourless pedant could condemn. It contained forty-two bedrooms and eighteen reception rooms—so Mrs Braxton had made it at the last recount. But Mr Braxton had not repeated with the interior the errors of the 4th Baron. He'd briefed the greatest expert in Europe with the result that that interior was quite tasteful and sublimely comfortable.

"Ugh!" he exclaimed, as they stepped out into the air, "it *is* getting nippy!"

"Yes," said Curtis, "there's a nor'-easter blowing up—may be snow for Christmas."

On getting back to the house Mrs Braxton went into a huddle with butler and housekeeper, and Mr Braxton retired to his study for a doze. But instead his mind settled on Lucky's Grove. When he'd first seen it again after buying the estate, it seemed as if fifty years had rolled away, and he realised that Abingdale was far more summed up to him in the little copse than in the gigantic barracks two miles away. At once he felt at home again. Yet, just as when he'd been a small boy, the emotion the grove had aroused in him had been sharply tinged with awe, so it had been now, half a century later. He still had a sneaking dread of it. How precisely he could see it, glowing darkly in the womb of the fire before him, standing starkly there in the centre of the big, fallow field, a perfect circle; and first, a ring of holm oaks and, facing east, a breach therein to the firs and past them on the west a gap to the yews. It had always required a tug at his courage—not always forthcoming—to pass through them and face the mighty Scotch fir, rearing up its great bole from the grass mound. And when he stood before it, he'd always known an odd longing to fling himself down and—well, worship—it was the only word—the towering tree. His father had told him his forebears had done that very thing, but always when alone and at certain seasons of

the year; and that no bird or beast was ever seen there. A lot of traditional nonsense, no doubt, but he himself had absorbed the spirit of the place and knew it would always be so.

One afternoon in late November, a few weeks after they had moved in, he'd gone off alone in the drowsing misty dark; and when he'd reached the holm oak bastion and seen the great tree surrounded by its sentinels, he'd known again that quick turmoil of confused emotions. As he'd walked slowly towards it, it had seemed to quicken and be aware of his coming. As he passed the shallow grassy fosse and entered the oak ring he felt there was something he ought to say, some greeting, password, or prayer. It was the most aloof, silent little place under the sun, and oh, so old. He'd tiptoed past the firs and faced the barrier of yews. He'd stood there for a long musing minute, tingling with the sensation that he was being watched and regarded. At length he stepped forward and stood before the God—that mighty word came abruptly and unforeseen—and he felt a wild desire to fling himself down on the mound and do obeisance. And then he'd hurried home. As he recalled all this most vividly and minutely, he was seized with a sudden gust of uncontrollable anger at the thought of the desecration of the grove. He knew now that if he'd had the slightest idea of Curtis's purpose he'd have resisted and opposed it. It was too late now. He realised he'd "worked himself up" rather absurdly. What could it matter! He was still a superstitious bumpkin at heart. Anyway it was no fault of Curtis. It was the finest Christmas tree anyone could hope for, and the whole thing was too nonsensical for words. The general tone of these cadentic conclusions did not quite accurately represent his thoughts—a very rare failing with Mr Braxton.

About dinnertime, the blizzard set furiously in, and the snow was flying.

"Chains on the cars tomorrow," Mrs Braxton told the head chauffeur.

"Boar's Hill'll be a beggar," thought that person.

Mr and Mrs Braxton dined early, casually examined the presents, and went to bed. Mr Braxton was asleep at once as usual, but was awakened by the beating of a blind which had slipped its moorings. Reluctantly, he got out of bed and went to fix it. As he was doing so he became conscious of the frenzied hysterical barking of a dog. The sound, muffled by the gale, came, he judged, from the barn. He believed the underkeeper kept his whippet there. Scared by the storm, he supposed, and returned to bed.

The morning was brilliantly fine and cold, but the snowfall had been heavy.

"I heard a dog howling in the night, Perkins," said Mr Braxton to the butler at breakfast; "Drake's I imagine. What's the matter with it?"

"I will ascertain, sir," replied Perkins.

"It was Drake's dog," he announced a little later, "apparently something alarmed the animal, for when Drake went to let it out this morning, it appeared to be extremely frightened. When the barn door was opened, it took to its heels and, although Drake pursued it, it jumped into the river and Drake fears it was drowned."

"Um," said Mr Braxton, "must have been the storm; whippets are nervous dogs."

"So I understand, sir."

"Drake was so fond of it," said Mrs Braxton, "though it always looked so naked and shivering to me."

"Yes, madam," agreed Perkins, "it had that appearance."

Soon after, Mr Braxton sauntered out into the blinding glitter. Curtis came over from the garage. He was heavily muffled up.

"They've got the chains on all the cars," he said. "Very seasonable and all that, but farmers have another word for it." His voice was thick and hoarse.

"Yes," said Mr Braxton. "You're not looking very fit."

"Not feeling it. Had to get up in the night. Thought I heard someone trying to break into the house, thought I saw him, too."

"Indeed," said Mr Braxton. "Did you see what he was like?"

"No," replied Curtis uncertainly. "It was snowing like the devil. Anyway, I got properly chilled to the marrow, skipping around in my nightie."

"You'd better get to bed," said Mr Braxton solicitously. He had affection and a great respect for Curtis.

"I'll stick it out today and see how I feel tomorrow. We're going to get the tree across in a few minutes. Can I borrow the two footmen? I want another couple of pullers and haulers."

Mr Braxton consented, and went off on his favourite little stroll across the sparkling meadows to the river and the pool where the big trout set their cunning noses to the stream.

Half an hour later, Curtis had mobilised his scratch team of sleeve-rolled assistants and, with Perkins steering and himself breaking, they got to grips with the tree and bore it like a camouflaged battering ram towards the ballroom, which occupied the left centre of the frenetic frontage of the ground floor. There was a good deal of bumping and boring and genial blasphemy before the tree was manoeuvred into the middle of the room and levered by rope and muscle into position. As it came up its pinnacle just cleared the ceiling. Sam, a cowman, whose ginger mob had been buried in the foilage for some time, exclaimed tartly as he slapped the trunk, "There ye are, ye old sod! Thanks for the scratches on me mug, ye old—!"

The next moment he was lying on his back, a livid weal across his right cheek.

This caused general merriment, and even Perkins permitted himself a spectral smile. There was more astonishment than pain on the face of Sam. He stared at the tree in a humble way for a moment, like a chastised and guilty dog, and then slunk from the room. The merriment of the others died away.

"More spring in these branches than you'd think," said Curtis to Perkins.

"No doubt, sir, that is due to the abrupt release of the tension," replied Perkins scientifically.

The "Families" met at Paddington and traveled down together so at five o'clock three car-loads drew up at the Hall. There were Jack and Mary with Paddy, aged eight, Walter and Pamela with Jane and Peter, seven and five respectively, and George and Gloria with Gregory and Phyllis, ten and eight.

Jack and Walter were sons of the house. They were much of a muchness, burly, handsome, and as dominating as their sire; a fine pair of commercial kings, entirely capable rulers, but just lacking that something which founds dynasties. Their wives conformed equally to the social type to which they belonged, good-lookers, smart dressers, excellent wives and mothers; but rather coolly colourless, spiritually. Their offspring were "charming children," flawless products of the

English matrix, though Paddy showed signs of some obstreperous originality. "George" was the Honourable George, Calvin, Roderick, et cetera Penables, and Gloria was Mr and Mrs Braxton's only daughter. George had inherited half a million and had started off at twenty-four to be something big in the city. In a sense he achieved his ambition, for two years later he was generally reckoned the biggest "something" in the city, from which he then withdrew, desperately clutching his last hundred thousand and vowing lachrymose repentance. He had kept his word and his wad, hunted and shot six days a week in the winter, and spent most of the summer wrestling with the two dozen devils in his golf bag. According to current jargon he was the complete extrovert, but what a relief are such, in spite of the pitying shrugs of those who forever are peering into the septic recesses of their souls.

Gloria had inherited some of her father's force. She was rather overwhelmingly primed with energy and pep for her opportunities of releasing it. So she was always rather pent up and explosive, though maternity had kept the pressure down. She was dispassionately fond of George who had presented her with a nice little title and aristocratic background and two "charming children." Phyllis gave promise of such extreme beauty that, beyond being the cynosure of every press camera's eye, and making a resounding match, no more was to be expected of her. Gregory, however, on the strength of some artistic precocity and a violent temper, was already somewhat prematurely marked down as a genius to be.

Such were the "Families."

During the afternoon, four engineers arrived from one of the Braxton factories to fix up the lighting of the tree. The fairy lamps for this had been specially designed and executed for the occasion. Disney figures had been grafted upon them and made to revolve by an ingenious mechanism; the effect being to give the tree, when illuminated, an aspect of whirling life meant to be very cheerful and pleasing.

Mr Braxton happened to see these electricians departing in their lorry and noticed one of them had a bandaged arm and a rather white face. He asked Perkins what had happened.

"A slight accident, sir. A bulb burst and burnt him in some manner. But the injury is, I understand, not of a very serious nature."

"He looked a bit white."

"Apparently, sir, he got a fright, a shock of some kind, when the bulb exploded."

After dinner, the grown-ups went to the ballroom. Mr Braxton switched on the mechanism and great enthusiasm was shown. "Won't the kiddies love it," said George, grinning at the kaleidoscope. "Look at the Big Bad Wolf. He looks so darn realistic I'm not sure I'd give him a 'U' certificate."

"It's almost frightening," said Pamela, "they look incredibly real. Daddie, you really are rather bright, darling."

It was arranged that the work of decoration should be tackled on the morrow and finished on Christmas Eve.

"All the presents have arrived," said Mrs Braxton, "and are being unpacked. But I'll explain about them tomorrow."

They went back to the drawing room. Presently Gloria puffed and remarked:

"Papa, aren't you keeping the house rather too hot?"

"I noticed the same thing," said Mrs Braxton.

Mr Braxton walked over to a thermometer on the wall. "You're right," he remarked. "Seventy." He rang the bell.

"Perkins," he asked, "who's on the furnace?"

"Churchill, sir."

"Well, he's overdoing it. It's seventy. Tell him to get it back to fifty-seven."

Perkins departed and returned shortly after.

"Churchill informs me he has damped down and cannot account for the increasing warmth, sir."

"Tell him to get it back to fifty-seven at once," rapped Mr Braxton.

"Very good, sir."

"Open a window," said Mrs Braxton.

"It is snowing again, madam."

"Never mind."

"My God!" exclaimed Mary, when she and Jack went up to bed. "That furnaceman is certainly stepping on it. Open all the windows."

A wild flurry of snow beat against the curtains.

Mr Braxton did what he very seldom did, woke up in the early hours. He awoke sweating from a furtive and demoralising dream. It had seemed to him that he had been crouching down in the fosse round Lucky's Grove and peering beneath the holm oaks, and that there had been activity of a sort vaguely to be discerned therein, some quick, shadowy business. He knew a very tight terror at the thought of being detected at this spying, but he could not wrench himself away. That was all and he awoke still trembling and troubled. No wonder he'd had such a nightmare, the room seemed like a stokehold. He went to the windows and flung another open, and as he did so he glanced out. His room looked over the rock garden and down the path to the maze. Something moving just outside it caught his eye. He thought he knew what it was, that big Alsatian which had been sheep-worrying in the neighbourhood. What an enormous brute. Or was it just because it was outlined against the snow? It vanished suddenly, apparently into the maze. He'd organize a hunt for it after Christmas; if the snow lay, it should be easy to track.

The first thing he did after breakfast was to send for Churchill, severely reprimand him and threaten him with dismissal from his ship. That person was almost tearfully insistent that he had obeyed orders and kept his jets low. "I can't make it out, sir. It's got no right to be as 'ot as what it is."

"That's nonsense!" said Mr Braxton. "The system has been perfected and cannot take charge, as you suggest. See to it. You don't want me to get an engineer down, do you?"

"No, sir."

"That's enough. Get it to fifty-seven and keep it there."

Shortly after, Mrs Curtis rang up to say her husband was quite ill with a temperature and that the doctor was coming. Mr Braxton asked her to ring him again after he'd been.

During the morning, the children played in the snow. After a pitched battle in which the girls lost their tempers, Gregory organized the erection of a snowman. He designed, the others fetched the material. He knew he had a reputation for brilliance to maintain and produce something Epsteinish, huge and squat. The other children regarded it with little enthusiasm, but, being Gregory, they supposed it must be admired. When it was finished, Gregory wandered off by himself while the others went in to dry. He came in a little late for

lunch during which he was silent and preoccupied. Afterwards the grown-ups sallied forth.

"Let's see your snowman, Greg," said Gloria, in a mother-of-genius tone.

"It isn't all his, we helped," said Phyllis, voicing a point of view which was to have many echoes in the coming years.

"Why, he's changed it!" exclaimed a chorus two minutes later.

"What an ugly thing!" exclaimed Mary, rather pleased at being able to say so with conviction.

Gregory had certainly given his imagination its head, for now the squat, inert trunk was topped by a big wolf's head with open jaw and ears snarlingly laid back, surprisingly well modelled. Trailing behind it was a coiled, serpentine tail.

"Whatever gave you the idea for that?" asked Jack.

Usually Gregory was facile and eloquent in explaining his inspiration, but this time he refused to be drawn, bit his lip and turned away.

There was a moment's silence and then Gloria said with convincing emphasis, "I think it's wonderful, Greg!"

And then they strolled off to examine the pigs and the poultry and the Suffolk punches.

They had just got back for tea when the telephone bell rang in Mr Braxton's study. It was Mrs Curtis. The patient was no better and Doctor Knowles had seemed rather worried, and so on. So Mr Braxton rang up the doctor.

"I haven't diagnosed his trouble yet," he said. "And I'm going to watch him carefully and take a blood test if he's not better tomorrow. He has a temperature of a hundred and two, but no other superficial symptoms, which is rather peculiar. By the way, one of your cowmen, Sam Colley, got a nasty wound on the face yesterday and shows signs of blood poisoning. I'm considering sending him to hospital. Some of your other men have been in to see me—quite a little outbreak of illness since Tuesday. However, I hope we'll have a clean bill again soon. I'll keep you informed about Curtis."

Mr Braxton was one of those incredible people who never have a day's illness—till their first and last. Consequently his conception of disease was unimaginative and mechanical. If one of his more essential human machines was running unsatisfactorily, there was a machine mender called a doctor whose business it was to ensure that all the plug leads were attached firmly and that the manifold drain pipe was not blocked. But he found himself beginning to worry about Curtis, and this little epidemic amongst his henchmen affected him disagreeably—there was something disturbing to his spirit about it. But just what and why, he couldn't analyse and decide.

After dinner, with the children out of the way, the business of decorating the tree was begun. The general scheme had been sketched out and coloured by one of the Braxton display experts and the company consulted this as they worked, which they did rather silently; possibly Mr Braxton's palpable anxiety somewhat affected them.

Pamela stayed behind after the others had left the ballroom to put some finishing touches to her section of the tree. When she rejoined the others she was looking rather white and tight-lipped. She said goodnight a shade abruptly and went to her room. Walter, a very, very good husband, quickly joined her.

"Anything the matter, old girl?" he asked anxiously.

"Yes," replied Pamela, "I'm frightened."

"Frightened! What d'you mean?"

"You'll think it's all rot, but I'll tell you. When you'd all left the ballroom, I suddenly felt very uneasy—you know the sort of feeling when one keeps on looking round and can't concentrate. However, I stuck at it. I was a little way up the steps when I heard a sharp hiss from above me in the tree. I jumped back to the floor and looked up, now, of course, you won't believe me, but the trunk of the tree was moving—it was like the coils of a snake writhing upward, and there was something at the top of the tree, horrid looking, peering at me. I know you won't believe me."

Walter didn't, but he also didn't know what to make of it. "I know what happened!" he improvised slightly. "You'd been staring in at that trunk for nearly two hours and you got dizzy—like staring at the sun on the sea; and that snow dazzle this afternoon helped it. You've heard of snow-blindness—something like that, it still echoes from the retina or whatever. . . ."

"You think it might have been that?"

"I'm sure of it."

"And that horrible head?"

"Well, as George put it rather brightly, I don't think some of those figures on the lamps should get a 'U' certificate. There's the wolf to which he referred, and the witch."

"Which witch?" laughed Pamela a little hysterically. "I didn't notice one."

"I did. I was working just near it, at least, I suppose it's meant to be a witch. A figure in black squinting round from behind a tree. As a matter of fact fairies never seemed all fun and frolic to me, there's often something diabolical about them—or rather casually cruel. Disney knows that."

"Yes, there is," agreed Pamela. "So you think that's all there was to it?"

"I'm certain. One's eyes can play tricks on one."

"Yes," said Pamela, "I know what you mean, as if they saw what one knew wasn't there or was different. Though who would 'one' be then?"

"Oh, don't ask me that sort of question!" laughed Walter. "Probably Master Gregory will be able to tell you in a year or two."

"He's a nice little boy, really," protested Pamela. "Gloria just spoils him and it's natural."

"I know he is, it's not his fault, but they will *force* him. Look at that snowman—and staying behind to do it. A foul looking thing!"

"Perhaps his eyes played funny tricks with him," said Pamela.

"What d'you mean by that?"

"I don't know why I said it," said Pamela, frowning. "Sort of echo, I suppose. Let's go to bed."

Walter kissed her gently but fervently, as he loved her. He was a one-lady's man and had felt a bit nervous about her for a moment or two.

Was the house a little cooler? wondered Mr Braxton, as he was undressing, or was it that he was getting more used to it? He was now convinced there was something wrong with the installation; he'd get an expert down. Meanwhile they must stick it. He yawned, wondered how Curtis was, and switched off the light.

Soon all the occupants were at rest and the great house swinging silently against the stars. *Should* have been at rest, rather, for one and all recalled that night with reluctance and dread. Their dreams were harsh and unhallowed, yet oddly related, being concerned with dim, uncertain and yet somehow urgent happenings in and around the house, as though some thing or things were stirring while they slept and communicated their motions to their dreaming consciousness. They awoke tired with a sense of unaccountable malaise.

Mrs Curtis rang up during breakfast and her voice revealed her distress. Timothy was delirious and much worse. The doctor was coming at ten-thirty.

Mr and Mrs Braxton decided to go over there, and sent for the car. Knowles was waiting just outside the house when they arrived.

"He's very bad," he said quietly. "I've sent for two nurses and Sir Arthur Galley; I want another opinion. Has he had some trouble with a tree?"

"Trouble with a tree!" said Mr Braxton, his nerves giving a flick.

"Yes, it's probably just a haphazard, irrational idea of delirium, but he continually fusses about some tree."

"How bad is he?" asked Mrs Braxton.

The doctor frowned. "I wish I knew. I'm fairly out of my depth. He's keeping up his strength fairly well, but he can't go on like this."

"As bad as that!" exclaimed Mr Braxton.

"I'm very much afraid so. I'm anxiously awaiting Sir Arthur's verdict. By the way, that cowman is very ill indeed; I'm sending him into hospital."

"What happened to him?" asked Mr Braxton, absently, his mind on Curtis.

"Apparently a branch of your Christmas tree snapped back at him and struck his face. Blood poisoning set in almost at once."

Mr Braxton felt that tremor again, but merely nodded.

"I was just wondering if there might be

some connection between the two, that Curtis is blaming himself for the accident. Seems an absurd idea, but judging from his ravings he appears to think he is lashed to some tree and that the great heat he feels comes from it."

They went into the house and did their best to comfort and reassure Mrs Curtis, instructed Knowles to ring up as soon as Sir Arthur's verdict was known, and then drove home.

The children had just come in from playing in the snow.

"Grandpa, the snowman's melted," said Paddy. "Did it thaw in the night?"

"Must have done," replied Mr Braxton, forcing a smile.

"Come and look, Grandpa," persisted Paddy, "there's nothing left of it."

"Grandpa doesn't want to be bothered," said Mary, noticing his troubled face.

"I'll come," said Mr Braxton. When he reached the site of the snowman his thoughts were still elsewhere, but his mind quickly re-focused itself, for he was faced with something a little strange. Not a vestige of the statue remained, though the snow was frozen crisp and crunched hard beneath their feet; and yet that snowman was completely obliterated and where it had stood was a circle of bare, brown grass.

"It must have thawed in the night and then frozen again," he said uncertainly.

"Then why—" began Paddy.

"Don't bother Grandpa," said Mary sharply. "He's told you what happened."

They wandered off toward the heavy, hurrying river.

"Are those dog-paw marks?" asked Phyllis.

That reminded Mr Braxton. He peered down. "Yes," he replied. "And I bet they're those of that brute of an Alsatian; it must be a colossal beast."

"And it must have paws like a young bear," laughed Mary. "They're funny dogs, sort of Jekyll and Hydes. I rather adore them."

"You wouldn't adore this devil. He's all Hyde." (I'm in the wrong mood for these festivities, he thought irritably.)

During the afternoon George and Walter took the kids to a cinema in Oxford; the others finished the decoration of the tree.

The presents, labelled with the names of their recipients, were arranged on tables round the room and the huge cracker, ten feet long and forty inches in circumference, was placed on its gaily decorated trestle near the tree. Just as the job was finished, Mary did a three-quarters faint, but was quickly revived with brandy.

"It's the simply ghastly heat in the house!" exclaimed Gloria who was not looking too grand herself. "The installation must be completely diseased. Ours always works perfectly." Mary had her dinner in bed and Jack came up to her immediately after he had finished his.

"How are you feeling, darling?" he asked.

"Oh, I'm all right."

"It was just the heat, of course?"

"Oh, yes," replied Mary with rather forced emphasis.

"Scared you a bit, going off like that?" suggested Jack, regarding her rather sharply.

"I'm quite all right, thank you," said Mary in the tone she always adopted when she'd had enough of a subject. "I'd like to rest. Switch off the light."

But when Jack had gone, she didn't close her eyes, but lay on her back staring up at the faint outline of the ceiling. She frowned and lightly chewed the little finger of her left hand, a habit of hers when unpleasantly puzzled. Mary, like most people of strong character and limited imagination, hated to be puzzled. Everything she considered ought to have a simple explanation if one tried hard enough to find it. But how could one explain this odd thing that had happened to her? Besides the grandiose gifts on the tables which bore a number, as well as the recipient's name, a small present for everyone was hung on the tree. This also bore a number, the same one as the lordly gift, so easing the Braxton's task of handing these out to the right people. Mary had just fixed Curtis's label to a cigarette lighter and tied it on the tree when it swung on its silk thread, so that the back of the card was visible; and on it was this inscription: "Died, December 25th, 1938." It spun away again and back and the inscription was no longer there.

Now Mary came of a family which rather prided itself on being unimaginative. Her father had confined his flights of fancy to the annual meeting of his shareholders, while, to her mother, imagination and mendacity were at least first cousins. So Mary could hardly credit the explanation that, being remotely worried about Mr Curtis, she had subconsciously concocted that sinister sentence. On the other hand she knew poor Mr Curtis was very ill and, therefore, perhaps, if her brain had played that malign little trick on her, it might have done so in "tombstone writing."

This was a considerable logical exercise for Mary, the effort tired her, the impression began to fade and she started wondering how much longer Jack was going to sit up. She dozed off and there, as if flashed on the screen "inside her head" was "Died, December 25th, 1938." This, oddly enough, completely reassured her, There was "nothing there" this time. There had been nothing that other time. She'd been very weak and imaginative even to think otherwise.

While she was deciding this, Dr Knowles rang up. "Sir Arthur has just been," he said. "And I'm sorry to say he's pessimistic. He says Curtis is very weak."

"But what's the matter with him?" asked Mr Braxton urgently.

"He doesn't know. He calls it P.U.O., which really means nothing."

"But what's it stand for?"

"Pyrexia unknown origin. There are some fevers which cannot be described more precisely."

"How ill is he really?"

"All I can say is, we must hope for the best."

"My God!" exclaimed Mr Braxton. "When's Sir Arthur coming again?"

"At eleven tomorrow. I'll ring you up after he's been."

Mr Braxton excused himself and went to his room. Like many men of his dominating, sometimes ruthless type, he was capable of an intensity of feeling, anger, resolution, desire for revenge, but also affection and sympathy, unknown to more superficially Christian and kindly souls. He was genuinely attached to Curtis and his wife and, very harshly and poignantly moved by this news which, he realised, could hardly have been worse. He would have to exercise all his will power if he was to sleep.

If on the preceding night the rest of the sleepers had been broken by influences which had insinuated themselves into their dreams, that which caused the night of that Christmas Eve to be unforgettable was the demoniacal violence of the elements.

The northeaster had been waxing steadily all the evening, and by midnight reached hurricane force, driving before it an almost impenetrable wall of snow. Not only so, but continually all through the night the wall was enflamed, and the roar of the hurricane silenced, by fearful flashes of lightning and raffales of thunder. The combination was almost intolerably menacing. As the great house shook from the gale and trembled at the blasts, and the windows blazed with strange polychromatic balls of flame, all were tense and troubled. The children fought or succumbed to their terror according to their natures; their parents soothed and reassured them.

Mr Braxton was convinced the lightning conductors were struck three times within ten minutes, and he could imagine them recoiling from the mighty impacts and seething from the terrific charges. Not till a dilatory, chaotic dawn staggered up the sky did the storm temporarily lull. For a time the sky cleared and the frost came hard. It was a yawning and haggard company which assembled at breakfast. But determined efforts were made to engender a communal cheerfulness. Mr Braxton did his best to contribute his quota of seasonal bonhomie, but his mind was plagued by thoughts of Curtis. Before the meal was finished, the vicar rang up to say that the church tower had been struck and almost demolished, so there could be no services. It rang again to say that Brent's farmhouse had been burnt to the ground.

While the others went off to inspect the church, Mr Braxton remained in the study. Presently Knowles rang to say Sir Arthur had been and pronounced Curtis weaker, but his condition was not quite hopeless. One of the most ominous symptoms was the violence of the delirium. Curtis appeared to be in great terror and sedatives had no effect.

"How's that cowman?" asked Mr Braxton.

"He died in the night, I'm sorry to say."

Whereupon Mr Braxton broke one of his strictest rules by drinking a very stiff whiskey with very little soda.

Christmas dinner was tolerably hilarious, and after it, the children, bulging and incipiently bilious, slept some of it off, while their elders put the final touches to the preparations for the party.

In spite of the weather, not a single "cry-off" was telephoned. There was a good reason for this, Mr Braxton's entertainments were justly famous.

So from four-thirty onwards, the "Cream of North Berkshire Society" came ploughing through the snow to the Hall; Lady Pounser and party bringing up the rear in her heirloom Rolls which was dribbling steam from its ancient and aristocratic beak. A tea of teas, not merely a high tea, an Everest tea, towering, skyscraping, was then attacked by the already stuffed juveniles who, by the end of it, were almost livid with repletion, finding even the efforts of cracker-pulling almost beyond them.

They were then propelled into the library where rows of chairs had been provided for them. There was a screen at one end of the room, a projector at the other. Mr Braxton had provided one of his famous surprises! The room was darkened and on the screen was flashed the sentence: "*The North Berks News Reel.*"

During the last few weeks Mr Braxton had had a sharp witted and discreetly furtive cameraman at work shooting some of the guests while busy about their more or less lawful occasions.

For example, there was a sentence from a speech by Lord Gallen, the Socialist Peer: "It is a damnable and calculated lie for our opponents to suggest we aim at a preposterous and essentially *inequitable* equalisation of income—" And then there was His Lordship just entering his limousine, and an obsequious footman, rug in hand, holding the door open for him.

His Lordship's laughter was raucous and vehement, though he *would* have liked to have said a few words in rebuttal.

And there was Lady Pounser's Rolls, locally known as "the hippogriffe," stuck in a snowdrift and enveloped in steam, with the caption, "Oh, Mr Mercury, *do* give me a start!" And other kindly, slightly sardonic japes at the expense of the North Berks Cream.

The last scene was meant as an appropriate prelude to the climax of the festivities.

It showed Curtis and his crew digging up the tree from Lucky's Grove. Out they came from the holm oaks straining under their load, but close observers noticed there was one who remained behind, standing menacing and motionless, a very tall, dark, brooding figure. There came a blinding lightning flash which seemed to blaze sparking round the room and a fearsome metallic bang. The storm had returned with rasping and imperious salute.

The lights immediately came on and the children were marshalled into the ballroom. As they entered and saw the high tree shining there and the little people so lively upon its branches a prolonged "O—h!" of astonishment was exhorted from the blasé brats. But there was another wave of flame against the windows which rattled wildly at the ensuing roar, and the cries of delight were tinged with terror. And, indeed, the hard, blue glare flung a sinister glow on the tree and its whirling throng.

The grown-ups hastened to restore equanimity and, forming rings of children, circled round the tree.

Presently Mrs Braxton exclaimed: "Now then, look for your names on the cards and see what Father Christmas has brought you."

Though hardly one of the disillusioned infants retained any belief in that superannuated Deliverer of Goods, the response was immediate. For they had sharp ears which had eagerly absorbed the tales of Braxton munificence. (At the same time it was noticeable that some approached the tree with diffidence, almost reluctance, and started back as a livid flare broke against the window blinds and the dread peals shook the streaming snow from the eaves.)

Mary had just picked up little Angela Rayner so that she could reach her card, when the child screamed out and pulled away her hand.

"The worm!" she cried, and a thick, black-grey squirming maggot fell from her fingers to the floor and writhed away. George, who was near, put his shoe on it with a squish.

One of the Pounser tribe, whose card was just below the Big Bad Wolf, refused to approach it. No wonder, thought Walter, for it looked horribly hunting and alive. There were other mischances too. The witch behind the sombre tree seemed to pounce out at Clarissa Balder, so she tearfully complained, and Gloria had to pull off her card for her. Of course Gregory was temperamental, seeming to stare at a spot just below the taut peak of the tree, as if amazed and entranced. But the presents were wonderful and more than worth the small ordeal of finding one's card and pretending not to be frightened when the whole room seemed full of fiery hands and the thunder cracked against one's eardrums and shook one's teeth. Easy to be afraid!

At length the last present had been bestowed and it was time for the *pièce de résistance*, the pulling of the great cracker. Long, silken cords streamed from each end with room among them for fifty chubby fists, and a great surprise inside, for sure. The languid, uneasy troop were lined up at each end and took a grip on the silken cords.

At that moment a footman came in and told Mr Braxton he was wanted on the telephone.

Filled with foreboding he went to his study. He heard the voice of Knowles—

"I'm afraid I have very bad news for you . . ."

* * *

THE CHUBBY FISTS gripped the silken cords.

"Now pull!" cried Mrs Braxton.

The opposing teams took the strain.

A leaping flash and a blasting roar. The children were hurled, writhing and screaming over each other.

Up from the middle of the cracker leapt a rosy shaft of flame which, as it reached the ceiling, seemed to flatten its peak so that it resembled a great snake of fire which turned and hurled itself against the tree in a blinding embrace. There was a fierce sustained "hiss," the tree flamed like a torch, and all the fairy globes upon it burst and splintered. And then the roaring torch cast itself down amongst the screaming chaos. For a moment the great pot, swathed in green, was a carmine cauldron and its paint streamed like blood upon the floor. Then

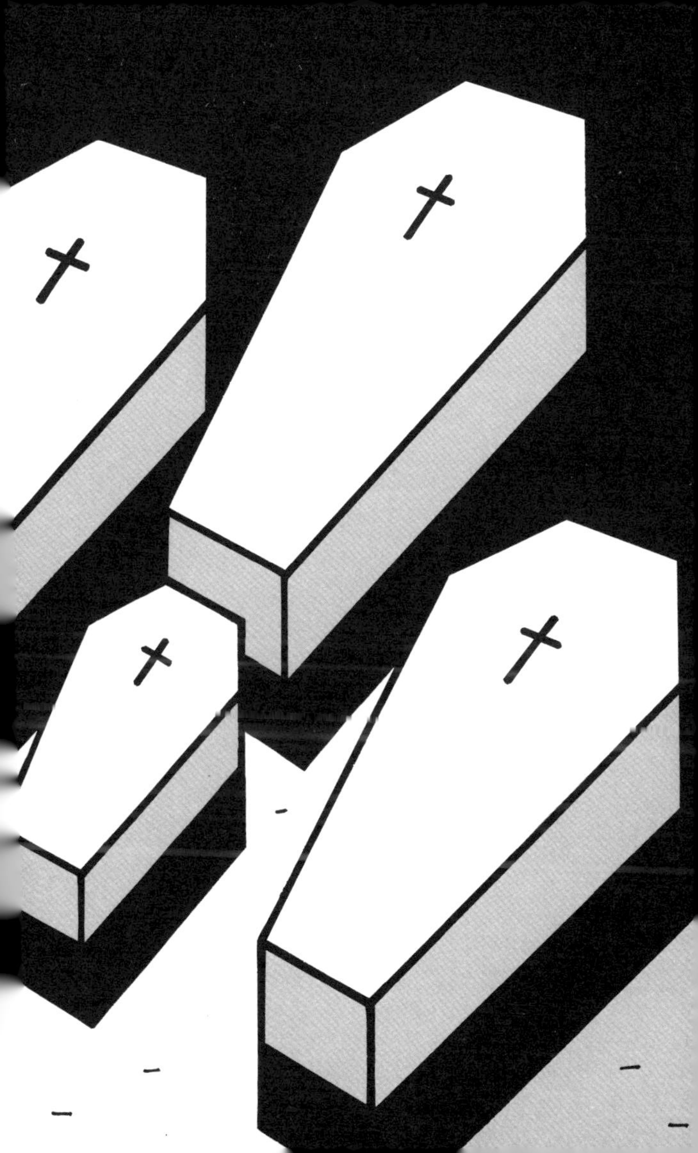

the big room was a dream of fire and those within it driven wildly from its heat.

* * *

PHIL TANGLER, WHOSE farmhouse, on the early slopes of Missen Rise, overlooked both Lucky's Grove and the Hall, solemnly declared that at seven-thirty on Christmas Day, 1938, he was watching from a window and marvelling at the dense and boiling race of snow, the bitter gale, and the wicked flame and fury of the storm, when he saw a huge fist of fire form in a rift in the cloud-rack, a fist with two huge blazing fingers, one of which speared down on the Hall, another touched and kindled the towering fir in Lucky's Grove, as through saluting it. Five minutes later he was racing through the hurricane to join in a vain night-long fight to save the Hall, already blazing from stem to stern.

H. RUSSELL WAKEFIELD (1888–1964) was an English author and editor, considered one of the greatest ghost story writers of all time.

ETH'S COMICS AND drawings have appeared in the *New York Times*, the *New Yorker*, the *Globe and Mail*, and countless other publications.

His graphic novel *Clyde Fans* won the prestigious Festival d'Angoulême's Prix Spécial du Jury.

He lives in Guelph, Ontario, with his wife, Tania, in an old house he has named "Inkwell's End."

Publisher's Note: "Lucky's Grove" was first published in *The Clock Strikes Twelve* (London: Herbert Jenkins, 1940)



Library and Archives Canada Cataloguing in Publication

Title: Lucky's grove : a ghost story for Christmas / H. Russell Wakefield ; designed & decorated by Seth.
Names: Wakefield, Herbert Russell, 1888–1964, author | Seth, 1962– illustrator.
Description: Series statement: Seth's Christmas ghost stories
Identifiers: Canadiana 20250253100
ISBN 9781771966733 (softcover)
Subjects: LCGFT: Ghost stories. | LCGFT: Short stories.
Classification: LCC PR6045.A252 L83 2025 | DDC 823/.912—dc23

Readied for the press by Daniel Wells
Illustrated and designed by Seth
Copyedited by Ashley Van Elswyk
Typeset by Ingrid Paulson

PRINTED AND BOUND IN CANADA